Hello, you!

Oh, please don't look inside the pages of this book.

Turn around and
quickly **run** ...

THIS BOOK BELONGS TO

SCHOOL OF MONSTERS

By Sally Rippin

HAIRY SAM LOVES BREAD AND JAM

Art by Chris Kennett

Kane Miller
A DIVISION OF EDC PUBLISHING

Today the school smells like a ZOO!

It stinks inside, and outside **too**.

On his own sits Hairy **Sam.**

Hairy Sam likes bread and **jam**.

Jam is sticky,
jam is **sweet**.

Jam gets stuck on Sammy's **feet**.

SQUELCH·

Sticky jam prints
up the **hall**.

On the carpet,
on the **wall**.

"Who has made all of this **mess**?

Was it you, Sam?
Was it **Jess**?"

"It wasn't me!"
Jess is **mad**.

Now Sam's in trouble.
Sam is **sad**.

Sam walks through
the garden **bed**.

Bob, their pet,
waits to be **fed**.

SNIFF
SNIFF

How will Sam clean
up this **goo**?

Oh! He knows just what to **do**.

Bob is hungry.
Bob loves **jam.**

Bob licks jam
from Hairy **Sam.**

SLURP!

Now Sam is clean,
but Sam is **wet**.

Sam can't go back inside just **yet**.

Sam thinks hard.
He'll save the day!

Sam dries off in Bob's old **hay**.

Now back inside for one more **job**...

... with his helper,
friendly **Bob!**

OM
NOM
NOM

Bob licks the walls, and then licks **Jess**.

He licks up all the
crumbs and **mess**.

Then Teacher Ted says,
"Good work, **Sam!**

You've cleaned up all that sticky **jam**."

"You've worked hard now,
I can **tell**.

But Sam, my dear, what *is* that **smell**?"

NEW WORDS TO LEARN
too
fed
Jess
mess
Can you point to words that start with s?
wall
mad
START HERE
NEXT LEVEL
WELL DONE

hay

Sam

sad

jam

sweet

bed

hall

goo

job

smell

wet

zoo

do

yet

day

Bob

feet

tell

HOW TO USE THIS BOOK

for adults reading
with children

Welcome to the School of Monsters!

Here are some tips for helping your child
learn to read.

At first, your child will be happy just to
listen to you read aloud. Reading to your
child is a great way for them to associate
books with enjoyment and love, as well
as to become familiar with
language. Talk to them
about what is going on in
the pictures and ask them
questions about what they
see. As you read aloud, follow
the words with your finger from
left to right.

Once your child has started to receive some basic reading instruction, you might like to point out the words in **bold**. Some of these will already be familiar from school. You can assist your child to decode the ones they don't know by sounding out the letters.

As your child's confidence increases, you might like to pause at each word in bold and let your child try to sound it out for themselves. They can then practice the words again using the list at the back of the book.

After some time, your child may feel ready to tackle the whole story themselves. Maybe they can make up their own monster stories, too!

Sally Rippin is one of Australia's best-selling and most-beloved children's authors. She has written over 50 books for children and young adults, and her mantel holds numerous awards for her writing. Best known for her *Billie B. Brown, Hey Jack!* and *Polly and Buster* series, Sally loves to write stories with heart, as well as characters that resonate with children, parents, and teachers alike.

① Using a pencil, draw 2 circles and a smiley mouth.

② Add a fluffy cloud up top, some bushy eyebrows, pupils, and 2 pointy teeth.

③ Draw 2 hairy lines for the body, with a rectangle at the bottom. Draw 2 more rectangles for wristbands.

④ Draw furry arms from the body to the wrists and 2 furry legs. Add a small line to create the shorts.

5 Draw hands and feet – 3 fingers, 1 thumb, and 3 toes!

6 Time for the extra details! Add horns, stripes on his wrists, and a belt. Don't forget the bushy TAIL!

Chris Kennett has been drawing ever since he could hold a pencil (or so his mom says). But professionally, Chris has been creating quirky characters for just over 20 years. He's best known for drawing weird and wonderful creatures from the *Star Wars* universe, but he also loves drawing cute and cuddly monsters – and he hopes you do too!

WELCOME
TO THE

SCHOOL
OF
MONSTERS

Have you read ALL the School of Monsters stories?

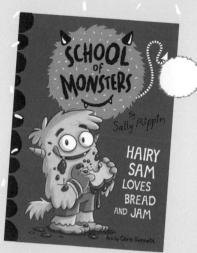

You shouldn't bring a pet to **school**.
But Mary's pet is super **cool**!

Sam makes a mess when he eats **Jam**.
Can he fix it? Yes, he **can**!

Today it's Sports Day in the sun.
But do you think that Pete can run?

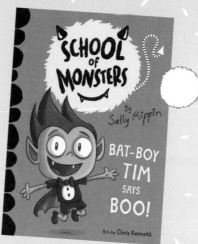

When Bat-Boy Tim comes out to **play**,
why do others run **away**?

Jamie Lee sure likes to **eat**!
Today she's got a special **treat** ...

Now that you've learned to read along with Sally Rippin's School of Monsters, meet her other friends!

Hey Jack!

Billie B. Brown

Down-to-earth, real-life stories for real-life kids!

Billie B. Brown is brave, brilliant and bold, and she always has a creative way to save the day!

Jack has a big heart and an even bigger imagination. He's Billie's best friend, and he'd love to be your friend, too!

Hairy Sam
Loves Bread and Jam

First American Edition 2021
Kane Miller, A Division of EDC Publishing

For information contact:
Kane Miller, A Division of EDC Publishing
5402 S 122nd E Ave, Tulsa, OK 74146
www.kanemiller.com
www.usbornebooksandmore.com

Library of Congress Control Number:
2020948967

ISBN: 978-1-68464-269-4

Printed in China through Asia Pacific Offset
10 9 8 7 6 5 4 3 2 1